Harvey's Marvelous Monkey Mystery

Also by Eth Clifford

Burning Star
The Curse of the Moonraker
The Dastardly Murder of Dirty Pete
Harvey's Horrible Snake Disaster
Help! I'm a Prisoner in the Library
I Never Wanted to Be Famous
Just Tell Me When We're Dead!
The Killer Swan
The Remembering Box
The Rocking Chair Rebellion
Search for the Crescent Moon
The Strange Reincarnations of
Hendrik Verloom
The Wild One
The Year of the Three-Legged Deer

Harvey's Marvelous Monkey Mystery

by

Eth Clifford

Houghton Mifflin Company
Boston 1987

Library of Congress Cataloging-in-Publication Data

Clifford, Eth, 1915–
Harvey's marvelous monkey mystery.

Summary: Harvey finds himself embroiled in a mystery
when a monkey appears at his bedroom window in the middle
of the night.
[1. Mystery and detective stories.   2. Monkeys —
Fiction]   I. Title.
PZ7.C62214Has   1987   [Fic]   86-20837
ISBN 0-395-42622-7

Printed in the United States of America

S   10   9   8   7   6   5   4   3   2   1

44173

This book is dedicated to the
memory of my Uncle Rudolph, a
master storyteller, and his son,
my dearly loved cousin, Alec.

Contents

1. In which a mystery begins   1
2. In which a statue moves   6
3. In which a girl screams   14
4. In which there is talk about blood   20
5. In which we say hello, good-bye, and welcome   29
6. In which a secret is discovered   37
7. In which Harvey blows the whistle   44
8. In which a father plays detective   50
9. In which Harvey sees red   61
10. In which a dog becomes a tiger   69
11. In which the eye is fooled   76
12. In which a clue is found   85
13. In which Harvey uses his marbles   94
14. In which the mystery is solved   102
15. In which a story ends   110

1
In which a mystery begins

I was having a nightmare.

It had to be a nightmare, because I knew I was in bed, sleeping, but my eyes were wide open, and they were fixed with horror on my bedroom window.

It was that quiet spooky time just before the sun comes up, when you think the darkness will never end, and nobody in the world is awake, except you.

In my nightmare, I couldn't tear my eyes away from the large branch of the big oak tree that just brushes against my window, where a *thing* was slowly swinging back and forth.

I didn't know what it was. It appeared to have a hairy white face and chest. I could even see its sharp teeth when it pulled back its lips.

I snapped my eyelids down hard. Then I talked to myself in a reasonable voice.

"You are having a nightmare, Harvey Willson. What do you expect, with Nora in the same house?"

Oh, yes. My cousin Nora was visiting us again. The last time she came, which was about six months ago, she got me all wound up in snakes. I was only ten then. I've turned eleven since that disastrous visit, but Nora has three more months until her birthday, so she's still ten. And she's just as peculiar as ever.

Not only was Nora in the same house, she was in the bedroom next to mine. My sister Georgeann moved in with a friend for the ten days Nora will be with us.

Trust Georgeann to make it sound as if giving up her room to Nora was a great sacrifice. The truth is, she left the house with the biggest smile ever seen on a human face. She moved so fast to avoid running into Nora that her thick blond ponytail went whipping back and forth across her shoulders.

I guess you can see Nora isn't Georgeann's favorite person, either.

Not that Georgeann is perfect. She just had a birthday, too — her sixteenth. I used to think she was hard to live with when she was fifteen. But sixteen is even worse. She acts so superior all the time now because sixteen is supposed to be extra-special, and grown-up. She even hates to be reminded that she was a little kid once.

The first thing she said when she heard Nora was coming, after she rolled her eyes toward the ceiling, was, "Mom, no way am I going to hang around this house with two weird little kids in it."

"Thanks," Mom said. She's usually soft-spoken, maybe because both my sister and my father have lung power you wouldn't believe. But right then her voice had quite an edge to it. "I appreciate your loyalty and willingness to stand by and help out."

"Wait a minute," I interrupted, before an argument could get started between them. "I'm not the one who's weird."

"That's what *you* think, Harvey. Honestly, Mom. It's hard enough with one . . ."

"Go on. Say it. I dare you," I yelled.

Georgeann went on talking without once glancing my way. "He always acts like such a kid. It's embarrassing."

I hate it when she talks about me as if I'm not even in the room.

"Well, at least I *am* a kid," I said. "What's your excuse for all the dumb things you do? You ever hear yourself on the phone talking to Hank Clay? *Oh, Hank, honey,*" I said in a sugary tone.

"And you expect me to stay?" Georgeann's voice was squeaky with rage. She reached over to yank my ear, but I ducked in time.

My mom gave us both a look that would stop a charging bull. Then she sighed.

That was yesterday, before Nora came. Now Nora was sleeping peacefully next door, while I was having this awful nightmare. What I ought to do, I told myself, instead of lying stiff with fright in bed, was go shake Nora awake. Why should I be the only one who was scared? The *thing*, whatever it was, probably had come for Nora, not me. She's the one with the case of the weirds.

Suddenly there was a loud *rat-tat-tat* on the window pane. It was the *thing*, knocking real hard, pointing to the bottom of the window. It couldn't get into the room because the window was only open a crack.

"I'm dreaming all right," I said out loud. At least I thought I said it out loud. Maybe that was part of the nightmare, too. Sometimes I dream in color, but I never had a nightmare with *sound* before.

I sat up and rubbed the goosebumps on my arms. The thing didn't go away, even though I knew I was awake now. It wasn't a nightmare after all.

There really was some kind of creature out there.

2
In which
a statue moves

I decided I ought to be sensible and get my
dad, or at least go next door and get Nora in
to share my fright. One thing I did know for
sure — I didn't want *it*, whatever it was, in
my room. Just as I started out the door,
though, the banging began again.

"Harvey," I told myself, "*shut the window*."
That thought was like a scream in my mind.
So I stretched out on the floor, the way sol-
diers do in the movies when they're inching
forward in enemy territory, and used my el-
bows and knees to reach the window. When I
did, I edged my hands up to slam the window
down.

"Don't look up, Harvey." That was the
good advice I gave myself. Did I listen? I

couldn't! I covered my face with my hand, but I spread my fingers apart and peered through, just the way I do when I'm looking at a creepy movie.

And that's when I really saw what the thing was.

A tiny black-furred monkey was clutching the branch of the tree. He had a cap of black fur on his head, but his face and chest were white. He gave me a mournful glance out of the roundest, saddest brown eyes I've ever seen. They were even sadder than Butch's eyes — Butch is my dog — and it's hard to get much sadder than that.

When the monkey saw me at the window, he was so excited, he wrapped his tail around the branch and swung free, upside down. Then he turned right side up again, and waited expectantly, meanwhile making the same small gruff sounds Butch does when he gets impatient with Doolittle, the cat that lives next door.

Butch and Doolittle are friends, if you can imagine a friendship between a big, old, fat dog whose biggest ambition is to sleep when he isn't begging for food, and a small, skinny cat with mismatched eyes — one green, one blue — and a head that bobs from side to side all the time, as if Butch is telling him something important and Doolittle is nodding, "I know, I know."

Butch was asleep under the bed. He was no help. He'd be insulted if I dragged him out before his nose told him breakfast was ready.

Even as I decided to open the window, I asked myself, "What am I doing? Suppose the monkey bites me." My dad says small animals sometimes act mean and scrappy just to make up for their size.

Well, the problem was soon settled. That little creature wasn't looking for a fight. He just scrambled over the sill, jumped on my shoulder, and snuggled against me with his arms wound around my neck. I could hear his heart pounding — ker-*boom*, ker-*boom*.

After a couple of minutes, he leaned back to look at me, a long, searching look. Maybe he was worried that *I* was going to bite *him*!

He must have decided to trust me, because he laid his face against mine, all the while making a small sound in his throat, like a young owl trying out its first hoot.

"Hoo," the monkey said. "Hoooo."

It was low and soft, as if the monkey knew everyone was still asleep in the house. Just the same, Butch moved enough to stick his head out from under the bed. He blinked up at the monkey, and made a growling sound, but his heart wasn't in it. I suppose he figured I didn't seem to be in danger, and with his poor eyesight he might have thought I was holding a stuffed animal, the kind he sniffs at in my sister's room.

The poor little creature in my arms was still shivering with fright.

"Hey, listen," I said, stroking his fur. "That's just Butch. He won't hurt you."

The monkey shook his head, to show me I didn't understand. Then he tapped me gently and pointed to the window. When I didn't move, he tapped me again, a little harder.

"Okay. Okay. I get the message. You want me to look out, right?"

"Hooo," he said, staring at me as if I wasn't the brightest human he'd ever met.

I didn't want to go to the window. How did I know what I was going to see?

Talk about losing patience. The monkey

pulled his lips back, showed me each and every tooth, and twittered, a whole series of high, fast chirps.

I imagined that was his way of saying, don't just stand there! Do something!

So I did.

Standing half-hidden in the curtain, I peered outside. Then I sneaked over to the other side of the window. After that, I was bolder. I stuck my head out, moving my head from right to left and back again, real slow and easy, so I wouldn't miss anything.

There was nothing there to explain why the monkey had been trembling so hard. Just as I was about to step back and close the window, I saw some leaves quivering on one of the low-hanging branches. Then I spotted him. A man was half in, half out of the shadow of the tree.

At first I thought it might be Hank Clay, trying not to let me see him. Hank is my sister's special boyfriend. Sometimes he comes around after he thinks everyone is asleep, and throws pebbles at Georgeann's window. Then they have a really sappy conversation, with Georgeann hanging out the window, and

Hank trying to keep his voice down to a quiet shout. He's sixteen, too.

If that's what happens when you turn sixteen, I think I'll skip that year and go right on to seventeen.

But it wasn't Hank. This man was short and chunky. His body was so rigid, he could have been a statue. Then, suddenly, he moved. Some small nighttime sound made him whip his head around and listen hard. I could almost feel the tense vibrations he was sending out. I was as scared as if a statue really had come to life.

He came fully out of the shadow of the tree then. I could tell, from the way his shirt tightened across his arms, that he had powerful, bulging muscles. He stared up at me, as if he wanted to memorize my face.

Our next-door neighbor Mrs. Motley — she's the lady that Doolittle owns — had told my parents that a prowler was loose in the neighborhood.

Butch must have sensed how I felt, because next thing I knew he was out from under the bed and standing beside me. His ears pointed straight up and he growled way back deep in his throat. He even tried to look menacing. That's very hard for a dog whose most exciting adventure was when Doolittle swung on his tail. But the man could see Butch all right.

Knowing Butch probably looked ferocious gave me courage. So I yelled down, "Hey you! You better get away from here before I call the cops."

Just then the first streak of morning light brightened the sky. I could see the man more clearly now. My heart began to skip around in my chest. I wanted to swallow but couldn't. The man's stony eyes had the mean look of a crocodile.

The next thing I knew, he opened his hands and let something fall. Then, in a rage, he slammed his fist hard into the open palm of his other hand, gave me one last cold look, and disappeared.

I locked my window, the monkey still wrapped around me, then walked back to my bed. Automatically, I began to stroke his body, gently, until I could feel him calm down.

Butch came back to the bed, too. He nudged me. Finally, a little curious at last, he

came close enough to examine the monkey.
Butch was puzzled. I could see that. He was
also surprised when the monkey suddenly
leaned over and tweaked the hair on his head.
Butch didn't seem to mind; I suppose he
thought the monkey was a new kind of Doolittle. So he relaxed.

Not me, though, for I kept wondering what
the connection was between that silent threat-
ening man under the tree and the scared animal clinging to me.

The thought that the man with the crocodile eyes might come back chilled me right
down to the bone.

3
In which
a girl screams

I was surprised that Nora hadn't rushed into my room when I yelled down at the man below. After all, her room was right next to mine. Then I decided I couldn't have called out as loudly as I thought. Certainly my parents, whose bedroom was at the other end of the hall, hadn't heard me.

I held the monkey away so I could study his bright-eyed little face. He opened his mouth in what seemed to be a broad smile.

"What am I going to do with you?" I asked him. I knew my mom wouldn't let me keep him. She doesn't mind Butch. That dog is family. But a monkey?

I could just see her tightening her lips and

shaking her head, with that no-back-talk-from-you-Harvey look in her snapping black eyes.

It was too early in the morning anyway for me to think clearly, so I went back to bed.

"You can sleep here." I patted a place beside me. That's where Butch used to sleep when he was just a puppy. Now he'd rather stay under the bed, though how he squeezes his big body into that narrow space is a mystery to me.

My eyes began to close. Before I could settle down to a couple more hours of snoozing, the monkey yanked at my arms.

"Listen," I said in a firm voice, "settle down, and no monkey business, get me?"

He didn't like that at all and showed it by gritting his teeth at me. Here I'd just saved his life, and he thanked me by grinding his teeth together. So I tried my dad's act when he wants Butch to obey.

"SIT!" I ordered.

When my Dad says 'sit,' any animal within ten miles flops down, no matter what he's doing at the time. My sister says that's because my father speaks with authority.

Well, why wouldn't he? He's a judge in traffic court. When he bellows (he *hates* speeders), people listen.

But this animal had a mind of his own. Instead of curling up in a cozy spot on the bed, he grabbed my pajama top and unbuttoned every button with his long, slender fingers. I was so amazed, I didn't try to stop him. When he pulled at the sleeves, I even helped him.

"Okay," I said, when that was done. "Are you satisfied now?"

I didn't expect him to answer me. Just the same, I wasn't prepared for what he did next.

He glanced around the room, leaped off the bed, and began to gather my clothes.

I'll admit I'm not too neat, and maybe my pants shouldn't have been on the floor behind the chair and my shirt hanging from the lamp. But I wasn't expecting company, especially not a monkey making small, scolding noises at me.

He dragged my shirt along the floor. Then he hopped on the bed and insisted that I put it on.

"Listen," I said, when he tried to put my

hands through my sleeves. "I'm eleven years old. I can dress myself."

When I realized what I was doing, I hit my hand against my forehead.

"I don't believe this. Listen to me. I ought to have my head examined. I'm sitting here at a ridiculous hour in the morning, having a conversation with a monkey, who is treating me like a kid with sawdust where his brain should be. Go away!"

I showed him what I meant by giving him a gentle shove. He shoved back. He wanted me up, and kept at me until I had my clothes on.

"You're running the show. Now what?" I wanted to know.

I found out in a minute. He skittered over to the door, reached up, turned the knob, opened the door, wrinkled his nose at me to show me how easy it was, and went into the hall. I followed him quickly. The last thing I wanted was to have that creature walk in on my mom and dad.

He turned right, though, opened the door to Nora's room, and peered in. He jumped on the bed, stood up, using his thick bushy tail to prop himself up, and stared at Nora.

She never moved a muscle. When Nora sleeps, she works at it.

He made up his mind about something, because he rushed to the door like someone with an important errand to run. I tried to grab him as he went past, but he was too quick for me.

He investigated the hall, slid open a closet door, and moved on until he found the bathroom. Now I was too interested to stop him. I watched as he snatched a washcloth and a towel from a rack, then swung up to the sink. Still ignoring me, he turned on the cold water, wet the washcloth, wrung it out, turned off the faucet, and hopped down.

As he left the bathroom, I grabbed at him again, but he just scooted out of reach. I tried to yell at him without raising my voice above a whisper.

Try that sometime; I guarantee it will make your ears pop and your face turn purple.

He was off and running back to Nora's room, dragging the towel behind him.

I guess I should have awakened Nora, but

I was curious to see what that little animal was going to do next.

What he did was slap that wet cold cloth across Nora's face and begin scrubbing. To do that, he sat on her chest and leaned his face close to hers.

Nora's eyes flew open. She took one look at the monkey, with his mouth wide open and every sharp tooth showing, and let out the kind of scream you only hear in horror shows.

I was sure that scream had punctured my eardrums for life.

4
In which there is talk about blood

A good long scream is a real eye opener. Even before the sound died away, my parents came tearing down the hall. You could tell they'd come awake in a hurry, because Mom was trying to get her right arm through the left sleeve of her housecoat, and Dad was struggling with the rope he used to tie his beat-up old bathrobe. Even Butch was spurred into action. He only came as far as the door, though, where he managed one *woof* before he flopped down. Butch probably figures he's old enough to be a coward if he feels like it.

When I heard them coming, I stepped behind the door so they wouldn't spot me and the monkey right off. When Nora screamed, that poor little thing had sailed into my arms and held on as if he would never let go again.

"What is it? What's happened?" Mom asked. My mom has kind of an olive complexion so I couldn't tell if she'd turned white from fright, but she sounded pale.

Nora gave me a quick glance. I put my fingers to my lips and shook my head. Then I waited to see what she would do.

I have to tell you about my cousin Nora. She has kind of an owl face, with thick eyebrows over eyes that are big and dark and solemn. She doesn't look it, but she is the world's biggest prevaricator. That's a fancy word for liar.

Last night, at supper, when Mom said she'd have to do something about Butch's teeth, because his breath was strong enough to push the walls back a few feet, Nora offered to brush them.

"Back home," she began in that earnest tone she uses when she's about to tell a whopper, "I have this enormous hippopotamus."

She stared me down when I opened my mouth to argue with her.

"He's my favorite pet," she went on. "He lets me clean his teeth all the time. I climb right into his mouth so I can clean the back of his teeth, too. I'm not the least bit afraid, even though he's gi-mendous."

"Gi-*what*?" I asked. "There's no such word."

"Of course there is. You don't know all the words in the world, Harvey. It's *gigantic* and *tremendous* put together. Gi-mendous."

Mom and Dad both smiled, and Mom murmured something about Nora's vivid imagination.

"You wouldn't know the truth if it came up and bit you," I told Nora.

"Harvey, I'll thank you to remember that your cousin is our guest," Mom said, her voice getting sharp. She feels very protective toward Nora because Nora has to live with my Aunt Mildred, who is the champion nervous wreck of the world.

I didn't answer. What was the use? I was just glad that this time Nora didn't have to come to school with me because it was spring break.

Right now, however, I was glad Nora

couldn't help telling her tall tales. I figured maybe she would distract my parents' attention from the monkey.

"Nora," my mom reminded her. "I asked you a question. Why were you screaming?"

She gave my mom a wide-eyed innocent stare. "There was a monster on my chest. He was trying to drown me. I must have been dreaming."

Mom straightened out her sleeve problem before she said, "It must have been a lulu of a dream. If the blood in my veins were milk, it would have curdled."

"If a monster drowns you, your blood turns green. That's a scientific fact," Nora went on solemnly. "That's why I screamed."

I forgot my parents still hadn't noticed me. I blurted out, "That's the dumbest thing I ever heard. Green blood."

Too late I clapped my hand over my mouth. My dad crooked his finger at me. When he does that, I move, believe me.

My dad is a big man. Everybody in my family is big, except me. He has fair skin that goes with his white-blond hair and piercing blue eyes. Now his skin flushed red to match his robe because he was working up to a slow boil.

"And what, may I ask, is that?" my dad demanded, pointing at the monkey.

Remember when I mentioned that Butch might think the monkey was one of my sister's stuffed animals? My sister is sixteen and all grown-up, she says. But she has a whole collection of stuffed animals. She's been saving them practically from the day she was born. They're all over the place—on her bookshelves, and along the headboard of her bed, and even hanging on the pole of her floor-to-ceiling lamp.

"A stuffed animal?" I asked, hopefully. I thought it was worth a try. When I saw the expression in his eyes, I said, "Okay. It's a monkey. A real one. But listen, Dad . . ."

"How did that creature get into this room?" Mom asked in a cold voice. I could see she was remembering the time Nora and I sneaked a snake into the house. It wasn't a fond memory, believe me.

"Your mother asked you a question, Harvey," my dad pointed out.

Well, I knew that. The problem was, I was

sure neither one of them would care much for my answer. But there was no way out. So I explained everything, just the way it happened, including the man under the tree.

My dad got mad all over again.

"You saw a prowler and you just invited him to leave . . ."

"I didn't exactly *invite* him . . ."

He wasn't listening.

"Young man, if you ever . . . I repeat, ever . . . see somebody lurking around this house, you are to come and get me at once. Is that clear?"

"*I* would have. That's the first thing *I* would have done," Nora said with a lofty air.

"I don't understand any of this." My mom was following her own line of thought. "What was the monkey doing in our tree? Where did he come from? It's a long way from the zoo. Still, he may have escaped somehow. Is it possible the man was its keeper, Thor?"

"Not him," I said at once. "He was too mean-looking. And mad. And the monkey was too afraid of him."

"Why wouldn't a zookeeper just come to

the door and ring the bell? Why skulk around outside in the wee hours of the morning?" My dad was puzzled, and he wasn't enjoying it.

"And don't forget," Nora piped up. "Harvey said he had something in his hand that he threw on the ground."

"Then whatever it was should still be there," my dad said thoughtfully. He wheeled sharply on his heel, left the room on the run, and headed for the steps. I started to follow, but suddenly the monkey jumped out of my arms. He skittered across the bed and grabbed a tiny white teddy bear with huge black eyes from the headboard. Then he rubbed his face against the toy bear and made a sound like a sigh.

"Ohhhhh. Isn't that the cutest thing you ever saw?" I could tell Nora was turning to mush.

There's something you should know about her. She is a natural animal person. I mean she just loves animals — all kinds — except turkeys. She even loves snakes.

I thought the monkey looked cute, all right. I half expected him to pop his thumb in his mouth. But I knew my sister would have a fit, so I said, "Are you out of your mind? You want Georgeann to skin him alive? Put that back," I yelled at the monkey.

Clutching the teddy bear, he gave me a fearful look and fled to Nora, who just automatically hugged him protectively.

"Leave him alone, Harvey. Maybe he has a teddy bear where he comes from."

"How dumb can you get? A monkey with a *teddy bear*? Oh, never mind. I'm getting out of here." I raced after my parents, who had just gone out the front door. I turned once when I heard Nora running after me.

The monkey was wrapped around Nora's neck as if he had found a friend. Nora must send animal messages the way the sun shoots out rays.

By the time we went out the door and down the steps, my parents were already at the tree. For a minute, Butch thought he was a puppy again, and ran around in circles, distracting my dad.

"Out!" Dad commanded.

Since Butch knew he was already out, he

took the order to mean that my dad wanted him back in the house, so he trotted off obligingly.

"If that dog gets up on the sofa, I'll kill him," Mom said, but she was too interested in what my dad was doing to go into the house to check.

My dad had knelt down, muttered something under his breath, whipped out his handkerchief, and carefully picked something up from the ground. Then he examined it closely.

"What is it, Thor?" Mom asked.

"Well, we've solved one riddle, Joy." He showed her a jagged-edged rock. "This is probably what he threw down."

I got as close as I could without touching it.

"Dad!" My insides went all hollow as I spoke. "There's blood on the rock!"

5
In which we say hello, good-bye, and welcome

"I think we should call the police," Mom said in a firm voice. "I don't like any of this one bit."

While she spoke to my dad, I dropped down to search around the tree.

"Here's another one." I was careful not to touch this rock, either. "It has blood on it, too, Dad. He must have been throwing them at the monkey to knock him out of the tree."

Nora clutched the little creature closer. "Maybe he's bleeding under his fur."

"Don't touch him," Mom ordered as Nora started to poke at his body. "Let's just get him back into the house right away."

Dad didn't say a word, just tucked his handkerchief with the rocks in it into the top pocket of his robe, and headed for the front door. We followed right on his heels.

"What's Uncle Thor going to do with the rocks?" Nora whispered to me.

"Don't you know anything? They're evidence. The police can probably get the crocodile man's fingerprints . . ."

"Who?" she interrupted.

"That's what I call him in my mind . . ."

"I like that." She repeated it. "The crocodile man. That's real shivery."

When we were back in the kitchen, Mom spread a sheet on the table. Then she turned to take the monkey. For the first time, she suddenly noticed what he was holding.

"Very funny, Harvey," Mom said. "Put that bear back on Georgeann's headboard." She reached over to take it away, but the monkey had an iron grip on it. He pulled back his lips, making it clear that he was ready to do battle for his little stuffed animal. Mom knows when to quit. "Never mind. Just stretch him out on the sheet, Nora."

When he saw his bear was safe, he relaxed, and let Mom poke around in his fur.

Nora held his hand, all the while cooing the

way people do at babies sometimes. I thought it was dumb, but the monkey gave her a soft brown look, so I guess he liked it.

Mom felt her way through the fur slowly. All at once her fingers stopped moving. Then she carefully spread the fur apart.

"Look at this." Her voice was angry. Mom gets furious when animals are mistreated. "His fur is sticky with blood. Thor, hand me that towel. I want to wash this area clean. Harvey, run upstairs and get the antiseptic from the medicine cabinet."

"I'll go," Nora said.

"Do you mind? My mother asked me to get it."

I didn't wait for an answer, just made for the steps and ran up two at a time. I was real annoyed with Nora. That monkey had come to my window, not hers. I was the one who had saved him from the crocodile man. But now, somehow, she'd taken him over.

I had almost passed my room on the way to the bathroom when I spotted the leaves quivering on the branch that hits my window.

"He's back." That thought struck me with a chill. I could feel panic stirring in my stomach. "He must be trying to get into the house through my window. He's after me."

I clean forgot my Dad's warning. I forgot about the antiseptic. I did my war crawl again, on hands and knees, across the floor, keeping a low profile. I heard that on television a couple of times — keeping a low profile. I never knew what it meant until just now. It meant don't let anybody see you, not ever, especially people who stand under your window at night.

"That's a funny way to look for a bottle of antiseptic," Nora said from the door.

I fell flat on the floor, rolled over, and scooted behind the bed for fast cover. Then I practically hissed at her.

"Don't ever sneak up on me like that again. You scared me half to death. Why aren't you downstairs?"

Nora gave me her own stare. "You're acting just like my mom."

I was insulted. Her mother, who is my Dad's sister, is my Aunt Mildred. She's a tall, skinny, twitchy lady, the kind who screams and jumps if you happen to come up behind her quietly. For the first time in my life, I could understand why Aunt Mildred screams and jumps at unexpected sounds.

This was different. I had good reason to be scared. But my Aunt Mildred is afraid of everything, most of it imaginary.

"Just think what it must be like to go through life scared of your own shadow," Mom always says about my Aunt Mildred. That's why my parents encourage Nora to visit us. They feel sorry for her. They think it's good for her to come to a normal house, if you can call a house normal that has a girl like my sister Georgeann living in it.

"What are you doing, anyway?" Nora asked.

"Get down," I whispered. "Now. *He's* out there."

Nora dropped down at once, crawled close to me, and was careful to stay hidden by my bed.

"What's he doing?" she wanted to know.

"I can't tell. I didn't see him. I just saw the leaves shaking and the branch moving."

Nora started to poke her head up over the bed. "Nothing's happening," she complained.

That was okay with me, but I couldn't let

Nora think I was a coward. So I said, "Stay here and don't move." I stood up, rolled across my bed in one fast swoop, dropped to the floor, and made it to the window.

What I saw made me stand up again.

"Get down!" Nora yelled at me. "Are you crazy?"

I paid no attention. I was too busy watching.

It wasn't the crocodile man out there. It was Doolittle. He had found something red and shiny caught on the branch, and it puzzled him. His head bobbed faster and faster as he made short dabs at whatever it was with his paw. The thing moved, Doolittle drew back quickly, then lashed out with his paw again.

Nora had reached my side by this time.

"It's Doolittle."

"I know who it is . . ."

"What is it? What's he found?"

"Never mind," I said. "Just go get the grabber from my mom's closet."

She was there and back so fast I think her feet never touched the floor.

The grabber looks like a long pair of tongs.

Mom uses it to get things down from shelves she can't reach.

"Perfect," I said, opening the window. I leaned out as far as I could and edged the grabber into position.

Doolittle arched his back and hissed at me before he moved back just beyond my reach on the branch. Why do cats have such short tempers? He's stubborn, too, because he just squatted down to watch, the motion of his head making it seem as though he approved of the way I was using the grabber. I had a feeling Doolittle would latch on to whatever it was as soon as I loosened it. After all, it was his discovery.

The grabber locked on to the thingamabob, and Doolittle did try to take it away. But I had a firm grip on it.

"Scram," I told him. Doolittle meowed to let me know that there were plenty of hard feelings, then calmly jumped into my room before I could stop him.

"What is it? What've you got?" Nora was frantic to know.

I eased the grabber in through the window.

Then I freed the object and examined it.

Just then my dad spoke from the doorway.

"Does it take two kids and one adult to fetch one bottle of antiseptic from the medicine cabinet?" he roared at us.

"But, Uncle Thor, we found something. Look."

"It's a collar," I said. "It must have been torn loose when the monkey ran across the branch. See? Something is printed on it." I looked closer. "Aloha!" I exclaimed. "His name is Aloha. That's a funny thing to call a monkey. Aloha means hello."

"Or good-bye," my dad said.

"Or welcome." Nora's eyes were shining. "Aloha means welcome. And that's exactly what he is!"

6
In which a
secret is discovered

It was at that moment my mom shouted up at us from the foot of the stairs.

"What are you doing up there, holding a convention? What does it take to get that antiseptic down here?"

"We're coming, Mom," I shouted back. "We got held up for a minute because . . ."

"Don't because me. I want you down here now, on the double." Her voice faded but from what she said next, we knew she had gone into the living room. "*Off that sofa this minute!*"

The next sound we heard was Butch scuffling along the tile in the hall, moving as fast as he could to the kitchen, and safety under the table.

Doolittle recognized Butch's funny walk, too, because he sauntered right past me, his head bobbing, his tail so straight in the air you could have flown a flag on it.

"Why is that cat in this house again?" Dad wanted to know.

He still hasn't forgiven Doolittle for strolling across the bookcase in the living room and knocking over his jar of pipes. Of course it would be his best pipe that broke. Mom said it was also his smelliest pipe, but we won't go into that now.

I didn't bother answering. He knows Doolittle comes and goes whenever he feels like it.

When we went into the kitchen, Doolittle was already there, on top of the refrigerator. From that perch, he was yowling down at Aloha. From under the table, Butch remembered he was a dog and barked.

"Quiet!" Dad bellowed.

Mom wasn't going to be distracted. She had already snatched the antiseptic from my dad and was applying it to the wounds she'd found under the monkey's fur. That didn't stop her from scolding the three of us, though.

"I could have been upstairs and down, and cooked a seven-course meal, in the time it took the three of you to get me one little bottle of antiseptic."

"Don't you want to hear why it took us so long?" I asked. "Don't you even want to know what we found?"

"This better be good." Mom didn't seem too interested. She concentrated on dabbing the antiseptic on Aloha's skin while Aloha watched with a serious expression.

"A collar," Nora burst out. "The monkey's collar."

"His name is Aloha," I put in quickly, before she could go on. I gave her a dirty look. I was the one who spotted the collar in the first place, from *my* room, in *my* house. Why couldn't Nora let me tell the story?

"Does it have the owner's name? And telephone number?" My mother is a practical lady. She always goes right to the heart of things. I never even thought of an owner or a telephone number.

Dad had said he was going upstairs to get

dressed, and was halfway out of the room. Now he waited. Meanwhile Nora tried to grab the collar away but I held it out of reach.

"Do you mind?" It seemed to me I had said that a lot to Nora, and she'd only been in the house since yesterday.

While I examined the collar, Nora suddenly moved behind the monkey so he couldn't see her. Then she cracked his name out like a gunshot.

"Aloha!"

The monkey sprang up, turned, and made a chittering sound. He almost seemed to be laughing.

Nora was delighted. "My test worked. He knows his name."

Aloha, now free from my mom's hands, flew into Nora's arms. You should have seen the loving look on her face.

"Bibble-dee-boo," she crooned. "Bibble-dee-bibble-dee-boo."

"Bibble-dee-boo?" my dad repeated with disgust. "What in the blazes kind of word is that?"

"It's monkey talk." Nora gave my dad her serious - get - ready - here's - another - whopper gaze. "I was lost in the jungle once. A lion was stalking me. I thought I was a goner. Then this bunch of monkeys found me. I talked to them in their own language, so they saved me and brought me back to civilization. Aloha remembers that, don't you, Aloha?" She snuggled him against her chest.

I opened my mouth to say something real mean. Just then Aloha grinned up at her. Nora's face lit up.

"See?" she said, a triumphant gleam in her eye. "He understands every word. Banananananahoo," she whispered.

"Hooo," Aloha answered.

My dad tugged his hair. He insists that my sister Georgeann and I speak what he calls the King's English, though I've never found out which king that was. But here was his very own niece, standing in his kitchen, making up ridiculous words. Did he yell at her the way he would at Georgeann or me? No. He came back into the kitchen and said in a cold voice, "What is so difficult about finding a name and address, Harvey?"

"There isn't one, Dad, but I think I've found something else."

I'd been going over that collar inch by inch. In the center, the part on which Aloha's name appeared, was a wider leather patch that seemed held in place by a shiny button on each side. I was trying to unsnap it. By accident, I pressed down on one of the buttons. The patch flipped open, and a thin flat whistle fell on the table.

Nora picked it up, turning it round and round in her hands. Aloha leaned over her shoulder to peer at the whistle. Then he banged the teddy bear on the table, said 'hoooo' a few times and shook his head. Mom thought it would be a good opportunity to grab the bear, while he seemed so distracted. But Aloha screeched and Nora said, "If you try to take his bear away, I'll hold my breath until I turn blue."

Mom looked up at the ceiling as if expecting help from above.

"Never mind that now," Dad said. He took the whistle from Nora, staring at it as if he expected to solve the puzzle just by studying the whistle. "Why would anybody hide this in a monkey's collar? It just doesn't make any sense at all."

"There's more! Look!" Under the whistle was a small, thin sheet of paper, folded several times.

I opened it, and my jaw dropped.

My dad snatched the paper from my hand. He studied it in silence.

"Well, say something, Thor," my mom demanded. "What is it?"

Dad frowned.

"It's a code of some sort. Look here, Joy."

Mom leaned over to see what Dad was pointing at, and Nora and I crowded around him, too.

"Letters," I said, my voice hushed. "And dots and dashes. It's a secret code!"

7
In which
Harvey blows the whistle

"Dots and dashes?" Mom repeated. "It must be the Morse code."

"What's that?" Nora asked.

"You don't know anything, do you?" I told Nora. "*Everybody* knows what the Morse code is. I've known it practically forever."

Nora gave me a suspicious glance. She didn't want to ask, and I sure wasn't going to explain how I knew. When my sister Georgeann was my age, my dad taught her the Morse code. They used to tap out secret messages to each other at the table. Then they would look at each other and laugh. Well, my dad would laugh; Georgeann mostly giggled.

Mom never minded, I guess because my dad probably told her later what the messages said. I was only six then, and I felt really left out; it used to drive me wild. After a while, Dad decided it wasn't fair to me, so they stopped.

I thought Georgeann had forgotten all about it, but when she started to get dreamy about Hank Clay, she taught him the code.

You should have heard some of their phone conversations, peppered with dahs for dashes and dits for dots all mixed up. Without letting them find out, I studied the code till I could recite it in my sleep. Then one day, when they were having one of their usual nonstop talks, I picked up the extension phone and listened. It sounded so dumb, I had to laugh. The trouble was, I forgot they could hear me.

Georgeann told Mom later, when she had calmed down from a high scream to a low hiss, that I had snickered. What she said, word for word, was, "This . . . this MONSTER . . . this miserable hyena . . . *snickered*. During a very PRIVATE and *personal* conversation."

"It sure was private." I grinned at her. "You want to hear some of the things they said, Mom?"

"I do not." Mom spaced the words out in a

way that told me I was in big trouble. The look in her eyes warned me that I was about to receive swift and just punishment.

There are rules in our house, some of which can never be broken, not even bent a little. No one can open anybody else's mail, not ever! Or read it, or peek at it when it is open and just lying around, without permission. No one can listen in on a phone conversation on an extension. What you overhear when somebody is talking in the same room is allowed. And more stuff like that — anyway, that's how I knew all about the Morse code.

"Someone has adapted the general idea," Dad explained. "But I'm puzzled by the combination of dots and dashes with this odd use of the alphabet. Look here, Joy."

Dad tore a sheet of paper off the shopping-list pad Mom keeps on the counter and finally found the stub of a pencil in the what's-it drawer. (All kinds of things end up in that drawer, which Mom promises she will sort out some day but never does.)

Dad sat down at the table. "This is a sample of the Morse code, see?"

He jotted down some of it, like this:

A • —
B — • • •
C — • — •
G — — •
H • • • •
I • •

"Now look at the code we found. It just doesn't make any sense at all."

Aloha's code looked like this:

GM •
MCS — — —
DIC • • •
WMFH • — —
BP — • —
TLO • • — —

I had picked up the whistle from the table. Looking at Aloha's code over my dad's shoulder, and without thinking, I put the whistle in my mouth and blew one short snappy blast.

Aloha, who had spied the fruit bowl on the

counter, had put his teddy bear down and was peeling a banana. When I blew the whistle, Aloha fixed me with an intent gaze. He dropped the banana, jumped off the counter to the floor and went to the refrigerator.

The others hadn't noticed yet. I said, "Pssst. Dad. Look."

When Dad turned, my mom and Nora did, too. Nobody said a word as Aloha opened the refrigerator, reached in, pulled out a quart of milk and set it on the floor. We were still speechless when he leaped back on the counter, opened a cabinet door, and took out a glass. When he jumped down to the floor with the glass in his hand, Mom made a nervous gesture, as if to stop him. Dad shook his head at her and frowned, so she just clasped her hands and waited for the glass to shatter. But Aloha was careful.

The container had already been opened, so Aloha just tipped it over slightly and watched the milk as he poured it in the glass. Then he returned the container to the refrigerator.

Everything he did was so coordinated, we could tell Aloha knew exactly what he was doing. Finally he brought the glass of milk directly to me.

"*G M*," Mom said with excitement. "And Harvey blew the whistle once. *Get milk*."

"What a marvelous monkey," Nora shouted. "What a gi-mendous marvelous monkey!"

8
In which a
father plays detective

I didn't object to what Nora said. Aloha *was* gi-mendous. It was exactly the right word for him.

"He brought the milk right to Harvey, because he was the one who blew the whistle," Nora marveled.

I had taken the glass of milk and was just holding it. Aloha tugged at my leg. Then he clambered up into my lap, shoved the glass up toward my mouth, and said, insistently, "Hoo. Hoo." If he could have talked, I guess he would have said, "*Drink* it, dummy."

I got the message. When I finished the milk, Aloha clapped his hands. I half expected him to pat me on the head and call me a good boy.

"Come here, you clever thing," Nora crooned.

All this while, Butch snored under the table. He must have been puzzled about why we were all in the kitchen and not eating. When Butch is puzzled, he sleeps until the feeling goes away.

Doolittle arched his back and hissed when Aloha took the milk out of the refrigerator. After that, he settled down to watch. Cats are patient watchers and waiters.

Just then the kitchen doorbell rang. It was Mrs. Motley. She's a small lady, with wispy gray hair and bright brown, button eyes. She looks as though one good breeze would knock her over, but we know better. Dad swears that Mrs. Motley could move a mountain if she was in the right mood.

We all like her — even Georgeann — because Mrs. Motley is full of surprises. For example, she doesn't smile unless she's wearing her "church teeth." She calls them church teeth because she only puts them in on Sunday. She says she hates earrings but she always wears them because she doesn't want to waste the holes in her ears.

"I've come to get Doolittle," she began, caught sight of Aloha, and stopped in surprise.

"I didn't know you had a capuchin monkey . . ."

"A *what*?" I asked.

"So that's what it is." Mom looked thoughtful. "A capuchin!" She began to smile. "My mother used to take me to the park when I was about so high." She measured off some space with her hand to show us how small "so high" was. "An organ grinder used to come there with his monkey, just like Aloha, the cutest little creature, all dressed up in a red uniform with silver buttons. And a red cap to match. While the organ grinder played, and all the little kids danced, the monkey would go to the grown-ups, whip off his cap and hold it out for them to drop pennies in it."

Mrs. Motley seemed surprised. "So they had organ grinders here, too, then. Imagine that. There was many a time I danced in the street as a little tyke, too. These capuchins are very valuable, you know . . ."

"And clever," Nora interrupted. "You want to see what he can do? Blow the whistle, Harvey."

"Sure. Okay." I felt wonderful, and proud of myself. After all, I was the one who saved Aloha, even though I didn't know he was special at the time. "I'll try another combination."

I studied the code, then chose the *B P*, which was one long, one short, one long whistle. As soon as he heard it, Aloha shot up to the counter, picked up the phone, jumped down, and brought it to me. When the dial tone buzzed out at him, he made a cawing sound back at it, like a crow who's been chased off his roost.

"*B P*. Bring phone." Nora's eyes shone. "What a splendific code!"

"Splendific?" I repeated. "There's no such word, Nora, and you know it."

"What does it mean?" Mrs. Motley asked. She looked as though it was the kind of word she might like to use herself.

Nora ignored me. She explained to Mrs. Motley, "It's *splendid* and *terrific* put together. *Splendific* just says it better."

Mrs. Motley nodded her head. It made sense to her, but then Mrs. Motley could easily be a kind of grown-up Nora, I guess.

"This is an extremely well-trained capuchin," Mrs. Motley told my parents. "He must have been working with someone who is handicapped."

"A *monkey*?" I was surprised.

"Harvey's right," Mom agreed. "Why this little creature is no bigger than a minute."

"How big is a minute?" Nora asked, giving my mom her owl stare.

"I can tell you." Mrs. Motley dug into one of the pockets in her jeans. She pulled out a large paper clip, a receipt from the supermarket, a small plastic bag filled with red cough drops that had glued themselves into one big blob, and a tape measure. Mrs. Motley's pockets are like my mom's what's-it drawer. You never know what you'll find in either place.

"You hold him still," Mrs. Motley instructed Nora, "and I'll measure him."

Aloha didn't seem to mind, though he wanted to taste the tape measure to see what it was.

"Just three inches longer than a ruler," Mrs. Motley announced. "Fifteen inches."

"So a minute is fifteen inches long," Nora said with a thoughtful look. "That's . . ."

"I know," I interrupted. "It's splendific."

"I believe I've read about it." Dad squinched his eyes half closed, the way he does when he's trying hard to remember something. "Wasn't there an article, Joy, about a quadriplegic . . ."

"That's a person who's lost the use of his arms and legs," I informed Nora. After all, I am three months older than she is, so I know three months' more facts.

"I know what a quadriplegic is," Nora answered with some annoyance. "I look at TV."

"Well," Mrs. Motley went on, just as if no one else had said a word, "capuchins act as helpers. They can feed people, comb their hair, wash their faces . . ."

"He washed mine," Nora said with pride.

". . . open and close drawers, fetch things, turn pages in a book, all sorts of . . ."

". . . answer the phone," Nora broke in eagerly.

"He's an absolute treasure. When did you get him?" Mrs. Motley asked.

Mom was quick to explain.

"Oh, he doesn't belong to us." She sounded worried, now that she knew what a special monkey Aloha was. She turned to me. "I simply cannot believe there isn't an owner's name and address on that collar."

"Let me look," Dad said. He examined the collar again, going over it thoroughly bit by bit.

"Wait a minute," he exclaimed. "I think something's been scratched out here, near the buckle. Harvey, get me my magnifying glass."

For a change, I didn't have to be asked twice to do something. When I got the glass out of the desk drawer in the living room, and gave it to my dad, he went over the inside of the collar again, paying special attention to the space near the buckle.

"Can you make it out?" Mom asked. I could see she was itching to grab it and study the collar herself. She's not a terribly patient person.

Dad nodded. "I think I can make out the shape of one or two letters. But this glass isn't strong enough. If we could put the collar under a powerful microscope, we'd probably be able to read enough to give us a clue. Tell you what, Harvey. Get me my camera."

"You've got it," I said, promptly. "I'm on my way."

As I went upstairs to my parents' room, I heard Mom say wistfully, "Wouldn't it be great if Harvey was this cooperative all the time?"

"Let's not ask for miracles," I heard my dad reply.

Nora giggled.

That made me mad. "Well, you're not exactly Nora the Perfect," I muttered. She couldn't hear me, but it made me feel better anyway.

"What are you going to do, Dad?" I asked as soon as I was back with one of his cameras.

"We're going to proceed logically. We have the rocks, which may have fingerprints . . ."

"What rocks?" Mrs. Motley asked, but Dad doesn't take kindly to interruptions, so he didn't answer.

"We have a collar that identifies this monkey by name. I'm going to take some snaps of Aloha . . . hold him so he faces me, Nora. That's fine. Now, I'll need a picture of Aloha's code."

My dad is a camera nut. He has equipment you wouldn't believe. He'll take photos of anything, like an acorn nestling on a leaf or water running out of a tap. Now that he really had something different to snap he was walking on air.

"Thor," Mom said. "Is all this really necessary?"

"Absolutely. Now I have something to show Oaty Clark."

Oaty Clark is our chief of police. Dad knows him really well, even though he's a traffic court judge. My dad thinks the way most people drive is a crime, and Oaty Clark agrees, so they're kind of buddies.

"They have some elaborate equipment in the police lab. They should be able to decipher at least part of what's been scratched out. Maybe enough for us to locate the real owner."

Suddenly my mother gasped. "Thor. Look at the time. And I never even made breakfast for us."

My dad lives by the clock. Not even a splendific monkey mystery was going to make him late for work. He asked my mother to put the collar and photos in an envelope while he went upstairs to get dressed.

There was no time for breakfast, he said, when he came down. But he promised to have some answers for us, *possibly,* when he came home.

When he left, Mom remembered it was her day at the School for the Blind. She works as a volunteer at the school, reading to the students, helping them with homework, and giving music lessons. Mom plays the flute, and she has a real nice singing voice, too.

She started to go upstairs to get dressed, then turned back again.

"The prowler," she said, sounding stricken. "I can't go off and leave Nora and Harvey alone in the house with a prowler loose in the neighborhood."

"Mom! I'm eleven years old." I was insulted. Did she think I couldn't take care of myself?

"Prowlers don't prowl in the daytime," Mrs. Motley said in her positive way. "But if you're concerned, I'll stay until you get back."

"Mom. Aren't you listening? You heard

what Mrs. Motley said. Prowlers don't prowl in the daytime."

How wrong could I be?

I soon found out.

9
In which
Harvey sees red

"You don't have to stay with us, Mrs. Motley,"
I said as soon as my mom left the house.

Nora agreed. "We're not little kids."

"*You* are, Nora. Don't forget you're still ten.
I'm the one who's eleven."

I was right, wasn't I? After all, there's got to
be some difference between ten and eleven.
E-lev-en. It even sounds more grown-up.

Nora didn't bother to answer. She just did
something real sneaky. She came and stood
beside me, straightening her shoulders and
lifting her chin in the air, so I would notice
that although I might be older, *she* was still
taller by a good two inches.

Mrs. Motley noticed. She's a smart lady.
She stepped between us, put her arms around

both of us and said, "I'm starved. I haven't had breakfast yet. Have you?"

Now that she reminded us, I could hear my stomach start to growl. I'd had the glass of milk Aloha brought me, but no real food.

"You two sit at the table and I'll whip us up something elegant. I haven't cooked for children since I came over."

Came over for Mrs. Motley doesn't mean from her house to ours. She means England, where she was cook practically forever in a big old country house for a rich family. Of course when Mrs. Motley moved next door and my sister Georgeann found out about the fancy dishes Mrs. Motley had prepared, she went wild with joy. My sister wants to be a chef in an important restaurant some day, especially one with a French name. Dad's promised that she can study in a special cooking school in Paris, France, when she graduates from high school.

There's a big *but* attached to his promise, though. *But*, Dad said in his positive this-is-it voice, Georgeann has to be a straight-*A* student to the very end. Of school, I mean, not her life, of course.

"How can you do that?" I asked her privately. I was only being sympathetic. I mean, Georgeann has to get *A*s in every subject, even math. I never get all *A*s. I'm smart enough, but I know I'm not the greatest brain in school. When Mom gets mad at me, she says my best subject is lunch.

"I have a goal," my sister answered. "You're too little and too dumb to understand that, Harvey."

Of course when she said that, she was still angry about my listening in on her phone powwow with Hank Clay. I don't care. I don't think a girl should like an absolute stranger better than she does her very own brother.

Mom never fusses about breakfast. She feels if she puts cold cereal and milk and some fruit on the table, she's cooked a meal. Mrs. Motley poked around in the refrigerator, studied the canned goods in the pantry, and hunted for pans and beaters and stuff. I think she found stuff Mom never remembered she had. Anyway, before we knew what was happening, Mrs. Motley had pineapple corn fritters browning on the grill, and was doing something to eggs you wouldn't believe. She whipped them into a froth, poured them into a greased pan and, while we watched, drew those eggs up in a spiral until they came to a high point, like an upside-down ice-cream cone. Mrs. Motley's swirlers, she called them.

"Fan-TI-bable," Nora whispered in awe.

"Dig in," Mrs. Motley said, sliding her creation onto our plates. "What's that word again, love?"

"*Fantastic* and *indescribable*," I answered. I had the hang of how Nora put words together by now.

"It's too beautiful to eat," Nora said, but I noticed that she wolfed her breakfast down with the speed of light.

"I'll just tidy up," Mrs. Motley told us, when the food was gone. "Then we can get comfy in the living room, and I'll tell you stories about the things I did when I was a wee bit of a girl."

Comfy? I groaned, inside, where she couldn't hear me. Nora swallowed a grumble, too. We didn't want to hear stories about the olden days. We had planned to play a video game Nora brought me as a present.

"We'll have a nice, quiet day," Mrs. Motley added.

That was when the front doorbell rang. I started for the door, but Mrs. Motley held me back.

"Let me check to see who's there."

Nora and I followed her to the door. Aloha had done his share of eating, mostly nuts and bananas. For a little monkey, he had an appetite like Godzilla. Now Aloha was back on his favorite perch — Nora's shoulder. Even Butch, who had gorged on scraps from the table and had the glazed look of a dog who has found heaven, tagged after us. Doolittle was part of our little parade as well, riding on Butch's back, which is something Doolittle has been doing since he was a kitten.

Mrs. Motley opened the door as far as the chain on it would allow.

"Yes?" Mrs. Motley asked.

Our front door has two long narrow panes of glass, one on each side. The glass has a special coating. On the outside, the panes look like mirrors, and no one can peer in, but it's easy for us to look out. Nora went to one window; I went to the other. We peeked out. Aloha did, too. Then he said, "Hooo," several times.

"It's okay," I told him. "It's just some guy collecting or something."

The short, heavy-set man at the door was holding a clipboard and pencil. He wore a dark green uniform, with a matching cap. On his upper right sleeve there was a round patch with printing on it that I couldn't read. Another small patch was on the peak of his cap. Under the cap was the reddest hair I've ever seen. With the sun shining on it, his hair seemed to catch fire. His hairy mustache was the same bright red. He had rimless half-glasses that sat on the end of his nose. When Butch tried to sniff at him through the crack in the door, he stepped back a little, lowered his head, and peered up at Mrs. Motley over the glasses.

"I'm from the Department of Health," he said, pointing at the patch on his sleeve. "We understand you have a wild animal in the house. I need to see your permit . . ."

"What permit is that, officer?"

"A permit to keep a wild animal as a pet. A

certificate that states the animal is healthy and is not a carrier of a tropical disease."

Butch wasn't sure whether he should growl or bark, so he did a little of both.

"You ought to keep a leash on that dog," the man snapped.

"In the *house*?" Mrs. Motley was surprised. "What an odd idea!"

"Pssst. Mrs. Motley," I whispered. "Ask him how he knew we had a wild animal in the house."

My voice must have sounded louder than I thought, or else the man had extra-good hearing.

"The neighbor next door called us and complained, young man," he said. He moved closer to the door and tried to peer in, but I had stepped back.

Mrs. Motley is sharp. She said, still polite, "And which neighbor was that, officer?"

The man pointed right at Mrs. Motley's house!

"I can't stand here all day. I'm a busy man," he said, with an edge to his voice. "Fetch the animal. We'll check him out and advise you when you can pick him up."

"Yes, of course. You wait right here, officer." Mrs. Motley closed the door firmly.

I peered at him through the window. The smile he'd put on for Mrs. Motley was wiped clean off his face. He glanced around quickly, then stared at the closed door. His mouth tightened. He pushed his cap up a little, and I caught sight of his cold eyes.

It was the crocodile man!

10
In which a
dog becomes a tiger

"It's him! It's him!" I tried to keep my voice low, which is hard to do when you're as excited as I was.

Mrs. Motley nodded. "The prowler. I know. I smelled a rat as soon as he opened his mouth."

Nora clutched Aloha so hard he gave a small squeal of protest. "You're not going to give Aloha to that man. He's mine!"

I was just going to ask Nora how Aloha became her property all of a sudden when Mrs. Motley told her, "Give Aloha to that creature out there? Are you serious, child? I'd as soon feed a rabbit to a snake."

Either the crocodile man thought it was taking Mrs. Motley too long to fetch Aloha, or else he heard us talking. He put his finger on the bell and kept it there. Then he started banging on the door.

"Open this door in the name of the law," he yelled.

Mrs. Motley's face reddened. "How dare he! That wretched man. Shout at me, will he?"

I got worried. "Don't open the door, Mrs. Motley," I warned when she put her hand on the knob. Did she listen to me? Of course not. Who listens to an eleven-year-old kid?

She just flung the door open on the chain again and ordered, "Remove your finger from that bell and yourself from these premises at once."

"No toothless old hag is going to keep me from getting that monkey, lady." His voice was rougher than sandpaper. He put his hands on the door and shoved hard.

"Call the police," Mrs. Motley whispered to me. Then she braced her body against the door and shoved back. Remember I told you my dad said that if she felt like it, Mrs. Motley could move a mountain? Well, right now she was determined to keep him out. Every time the door yielded a little bit, Mrs. Motley pushed it shut again.

"Nora. Quick." I poked her and motioned her to follow. Nora knows when to argue, and when to do what she's told. Still hanging on to Aloha, she was right behind me as I went up the steps.

"Why couldn't we call the police from the kitchen phone?" she wanted to know.

I shook my head. "He'd be gone before they came. I have a better idea. Let's teach him a lesson." Before she could interrupt, I explained, "There's a pail in the cabinet under the sink in the bathroom. I'm going to fill it with water. Do you want to help me?"

She looked puzzled, but she said, "Sure."

It only took a minute to find the pail and fill it. Then we went into Nora's room, with both of us holding the pail by the handle because it was so big and heavy. We placed it on the floor under the window, which happens to be directly over the front door. I slid the window open a little bit at a time so it wouldn't make any noise.

Nora looked at me and grinned. She's got a quick mind all right. She caught on right away.

I grinned back. "Quick, Nora. Now!"

Aloha had swung himself up onto the stuffed animal pole near the window. Now he watched us with a bright expression.

"Heave ho!" Nora shouted as we tipped the pail out the window, right on the crocodile man below. The flood of water knocked his cap off. His red hair moved to one side of his head and hung from his ear. His mustache slipped halfway off his upper lip as well. He looked like a clown, with his hair and mustache all on one side of his face.

But he wasn't laughing. Soaking wet, he glared up at us with such a menacing air that Nora pulled back from the window. The man shook his fist at me and yelled, "You'll be sorry before I'm through with you two."

Nora shivered. "What an awfibble man!" Before I could ask, Nora explained, "It's *awful* and *horrible*, put together."

It made a lot of sense. He *was* awfibble.

Nora tiptoed back to the window, and we both looked down to see what was happening. The water had caught the crocodile man just as he had broken the chain and pushed the door open. He didn't get inside, though, because suddenly Butch made up his mind he was a tiger, and attacked. He stood up on his hind legs and hurled himself at the crocodile man, who tripped, caught himself, turned, and ran.

We could see Butch tearing after him, nipping at his heels, trying to clamp his teeth into a chunk of leg. The man's wig fell off. That didn't distract Butch, who is a very single-minded type of dog. But it did distract Doolittle, who ran behind Butch, hissing and spitting. Doolittle immediately stopped to investigate the wig, which must have seemed like some strange kind of animal to him. Then he attacked it. Finally, he carried it off in his teeth as if he'd caught the biggest rat in history.

Meanwhile Butch had grabbed firm hold of the crocodile man's pants, ripping one of the pockets open. A small black case fell out and hit the ground.

The crocodile man didn't stop, though, just headed for the van at the curb. Without bothering to close the door in the back, he leaped in and took off with the tires squealing. He hit a bump, and a small cage came flying out into the street, but he never looked back.

"Well," Mrs. Motley said, when we came downstairs again. "That was a splendid bit of work." She shook hands with Nora, then with me. Aloha stuck a hand out, so she shook his as well. "Did you call the police?"

"There wasn't time," I explained.

"Never mind. That evil man is gone now. I'm going to call your father. Then you two are coming to my house for the rest of the day, until your parents come home."

"He won't come back, not with Butch here," Nora objected.

"Probably not, but I still want you next door, where you'll be safe."

"Okay," I agreed. "But first I want to see what's in that black case . . ."

"And I want to get the cage so he can't try to put Aloha in it," Nora said.

She handed Aloha to Mrs. Motley, then followed me out the front door.

When we came back with the case and the cage, we found that Mrs. Motley had made herself some tea, which she called a *cuppa*.

"There's nothing like a cuppa to soothe the nerves," she told us, sipping a liquid so hot the steam seemed to be coming out of her ears.

Butch was obviously exhausted. He had flopped down under the table; the tiger in him was fast asleep. Doolittle was back on top of the refrigerator, nodding his head. Aloha was curled up on one of the padded chairs and making soft snoring sounds.

When I showed Mrs. Motley the black case, she put her tea down. Before I could stop her, and warn her about fingerprints, she had it open. Then she gasped. Nora and I were struck dumb.

Inside the case was a hypodermic with a long, wicked-looking needle, and a small bottle filled with liquid.

Mrs. Motley said in a horrified voice, "Whatever was that terrible man planning to do?"

11
In which
the eye is fooled

"Poison!" Nora's voice was hollow. "He was going to kill Aloha."

"No, he wasn't," I said. "Why would he try so hard to get Aloha just to kill him? It doesn't make sense."

"Then it has something to do with the code," Nora suggested. "Maybe the code has two meanings. Maybe he's an international spy and he . . ."

"No, child." Mrs. Motley was firm about that. "If a country had to depend on such a man to spy for them, they'd be out of the spy business overnight. Why, that ridiculous man couldn't even imitate a health official. No, take it from me, he has some other plan up his sleeve." She took a last quick look around to make sure the kitchen was in apple-pie order. Then she said, "All right. Off we go to my house."

"Wait," Nora said. She didn't explain but ran out of the room, taking Aloha with her. In minutes she was back in the kitchen again. She had wrapped Aloha in a small white blanket, and was cradling him in her arms just like a baby. Aloha looked very content, with his fingers clutching one edge of the blanket and his teddy bear nuzzling his neck.

Mrs. Motley and Nora cooed at Aloha on the way to Mrs. Motley's house. Of course Butch came along, expecting to be fed again. And though she looked at Aloha, Mrs. Motley hung on to Doolittle, holding his head tight to keep it from bobbing.

I knew what to expect when Mrs. Motley opened her front door, but Nora was struck speechless. See, Mrs. Motley hadn't lived next door the last time Nora visited, but I'd been in and out of her house a lot since then.

Mom says Mrs. Motley is an original thinker, but my dad says there ought to be a law —

one thing my dad hates is change. Mom can't even move a chair from one side of a room to the other without getting howls of protest from my dad.

But Mrs. Motley! When she'd first moved in, six months ago, she'd painted all her living room walls with street scenes. There were huge buildings, and crowded streets, and mobs of people coming and going. Dad went in exactly once to welcome her and came rushing out. He swore up and down it was the noisiest room he'd ever been in.

Mom loved it on sight. "It's like stepping through a window into another world," she told Mrs. Motley.

I agreed with Mom. I could almost hear what the people were saying.

Mrs. Motley explained it was called *trompe l'oeil*, which looks funny when you write it and sounds peculiar when you say it, but is only French for "fool the eye."

Three months ago I guess the noise got to be too much even for Mrs. Motley — city noises, I mean. Because she sure changed everything.

"Wow!" Nora said when she walked in. It was the first time she couldn't make up one of her special words.

On the living room wall facing the door, Mrs. Motley had painted a stormy sky, a restless ocean, and a beach with tufts of tall dune grasses here and there that appeared to be whipped over by a wind you couldn't see but thought you felt.

On one long side wall, there was another seascape, a quiet one, with the sun shining on a tranquil sea, and a small child, back toward us, digging in the sand.

"Stormy there —" Mrs. Motley explained, when she saw the way Nora's eyes shifted from one wall to the other and back again in a puzzled way — "when it's stormy here." She pressed her hand against her heart. "And quiet there —" she waved at the second wall — "when it's serene here." She pointed a finger at her head.

The third wall, which was not as wide as the others, had no paintings. Instead, it was decorated with a colorful fishing net. Here and there on the net were round, dark-brown floaters. Under the net, on the floor, was a real rowboat. Every time I saw it, I'd get a dreamy feeling that all I had to do was climb in, push off into the quiet sea on the next wall, and disappear over the horizon.

Butch liked the rowboat, too. He always headed directly for it. Then he would rest his head on one of the hard benchlike seats, as he was doing now. His eyes glazed over. Butch is the only dog in America who can sleep with his eyes open.

Doolittle curled up in the bottom of the boat. He's never too far away from Butch if he can help it. Aloha just clung to Nora and "hooo'd" a few times.

"Wow!" Nora repeated.

Mrs. Motley swiveled her head around. Then she waved her hand. "I've had enough of the sea. It has to go."

Nora was disappointed. "Why? I love it."

"I don't feel like water and sky anymore. I feel like jungle now."

"You mean those dark woods and enormous trees and tigers' eyes shining at you through the leaves?" Nora shivered. "It sounds spooky."

"And big colorful birds, and monkeys in the trees," Mrs. Motley said in a cheerful voice.

Aloha looked at her.

"That's right," she told him. "Monkeys like you." She clapped her hands, then rubbed them briskly. "Now then, Harvey, will you give me a hand taking down this net later?"

Before I could answer, Nora asked quickly, "What are you going to do with it?"

Mrs. Motley shrugged her shoulders. "Throw it away, probably." Then she noticed the expression on Nora's face. "Would you like to have it?" Nora lit up like a bright summer day. "Then you shall have it, child. Though how you will get it home I can't imagine. It is rather large, but maybe it will fit into one of my trashcan bags."

I could tell Nora wished there was some way she could take the wall paintings, too. She was lucky she couldn't. They'd probably send my Aunt Mildred screaming into the night. My aunt likes pictures of grass growing very, *very* quietly, or swans floating on a pond . . . stuff like that.

"Before we tackle the net, I must call your

father," Mrs. Motley said to me. She went into the kitchen. The minute she was there, Butch's ears perked up, and he was out of the boat in a flash. We'd just had breakfast a little while ago, so she wasn't going to feed him, but hope dies hard with that dog. Doolittle followed, naturally, his head bobbing again.

After Mrs. Motley spoke to my dad for a while, she called us to the phone.

"Harvey —" my dad had that positive, you-pay-attention sound he gets when he's giving me an order — "you and Nora stay where you are. You are not to move a muscle till I come home, do I make myself clear? I'll be back soon."

"Well," Mrs. Motley said, when I hung up, "why don't we take the net down now, while we're waiting?"

Not moving a muscle didn't mean being glued to my chair, I figured, so we all went into the living room again. It took less time than I expected, getting the net down, I mean. But Nora and Mrs. Motley got so tangled in it when it fell, I had a hard time freeing them. Nora didn't care. She still wanted it.

"Before I can even touch the walls," Mrs.

Motley told us, "I need to shift some things."

So Nora and I gave her a hand moving some of the smaller pieces of furniture into the hall and the back room she called her sewing room. Then I covered some of the furniture with sheets while Nora helped Mrs. Motley spread long plastic covers on the floor against the walls. The rowboat would have to wait for her handyman to move.

That was as far as we got when the front doorbell rang.

"I expect that will be your father." Mrs. Motley started to get up from the floor.

"He must have broken all speed records to get home that fast," Nora said.

"Not my dad," I told her positively. "The only way he'll speed is if he's in a police car. On police business," I added. "Don't get up, Mrs. Motley. I'll get the door."

I was too late. While we were talking, Aloha scampered to the door and opened it. Standing on the step were my dad and Chief Oaty Clark.

The Chief stared down at Aloha. Then he laughed. "First time in my life a monkey opened the door for me."

Aloha fled back to Nora. I couldn't blame him. Chief Clark's voice booms as if it's coming at you through a bullhorn.

"Is everything all right?" my dad asked, keeping his head down so he wouldn't have to look at Mrs. Motley's pictures.

Nora beamed. "Splendific, Uncle Thor."

"Fine. We can go back to the house now. Your aunt will be back in a few minutes, Nora. The Chief and I think we've found a clue that will tell us something about Aloha."

A clue!

We forgot about helping Mrs. Motley.

What could be more important than finding out about Aloha?

12
In which
a clue is found

So we paraded back to my house, animals and people, including Mrs. Motley.

"Aren't you going to get started on your walls?" Nora asked in a whisper.

"At a time like this? When the mystery deepens? The walls will still be here when this is all over, lovey," Mrs. Motley said.

While Nora was talking to Mrs. Motley, I showed my dad and Oaty Clark the black case. When they saw the hypodermic, Dad's face turned stormy. Chief Clark didn't say a word, just quietly tucked the case into one of his pockets.

As soon as we were back in our own kitchen, the Chief put Aloha's collar on the table.

He began to explain what the lab had done, but my dad stopped him.

"Let's wait for Joy, so we don't have to go over it all again."

"Mom won't mind, Dad. Please. We're dying to know . . . "

"Please, Uncle Thor," Nora begged.

My dad just said, "Coffee, Oaty?"

"Good idea. Now then —" the Chief turned to the rest of us — "want to hear the latest joke while we're waiting?"

Mrs. Motley nodded. So did Nora. But I sighed, being careful not to let the Chief hear me. I must tell you something about him. He must have the biggest dumb joke collection in the whole world. And I think I've heard them all!

The Chief started a safety program in our town back when I was in second grade. He's still a popular speaker in our school for two reasons. One is the way he sandwiches jokes into his talks about safety. The other is the Chief's Adam's apple.

Oaty Clark looks like a strung-out bean pole, with hair that appears to be borrowed from a scarecrow, wispy and shooting out of his head in all directions. He has small brown eyes, practically hidden behind scrunched-up eyelids that make you feel he's standing in strong sunlight and can't keep his eyes open. He has a long, thin head on a long, skinny neck, and in that neck is a big Adam's apple that bobs up and down when he talks.

In second grade I thought his jokes were funny, and his Adam's apple even funnier. I felt the same way in third grade. By fourth grade I was beginning to moan at his jokes. In fifth grade, I knew they were all dumb. But in fifth grade, Petey Warren and I had a steady bet going about how many times the Chief's Adam's apple would bob up and down during his speech. Chief Clark caught me counting and gave me a hard look, so I lost a quarter to Petey.

As soon as Chief Clark finished his dumb joke, Mrs. Motley drew a deep breath.

"Come on," he said. "It couldn't have been that bad."

Mrs. Motley is English, so she has good manners. She said quickly, "I was just thinking of the prowler. I do wish you could catch him."

Chief Clark looked surprised. "The prowler? We nabbed him two days ago."

"Then if the crocodile man isn't the prowler," Nora asked, "who is he?"

Chief Clark shook his head. "We don't know. Not yet."

Dad got up to give the Chief a refill on his coffee. I let my hand wander across the table to where Aloha's collar was.

"Let it be," Dad said, coming back to the table.

"I only want to look. There's no harm in just looking. It's not like you're telling me anything, Dad."

"Here, Harvey." The Chief pushed the collar closer to me. "Figure it out, and I'll put you in our detective squad."

Just then my mom walked in.

"Hurry and sit down, Aunt Joy," Nora said. Before Mom could ask why, Nora added, "They wouldn't tell us what they found out at the lab until you were here."

The Chief explained that the lab had managed to highlight some of the letters so they were readable.

"But where's the clue?" Nora burst in. She had examined the collar, too. "All I can see is a jumble of letters. What kind of clue is that?"

This is what it looked like:

```
          ort
        x    0
  V va        ana
```

I flashed Nora one of my best superior smiles.

"It's so simple."

"You're so aggranoying," Nora said.

"*Aggranoying?*" Dad repeated, shaking his head.

"It's *aggravating* and *annoying* put together," she said. "What's so simple, Harvey?"

"It's a name and address. Can't you see the way it's laid out? *Ort* is part of the name, the *x* and *o* have to be the house and street, and the *v* space *va* and the *ana* are the city and state."

"Big deal," Nora told me, looking disappointed. "That's what Aunt Joy asked you to look for when we first found the collar. Where's the clue?"

We? I was the one who found it. All right, Doolittle did, but I knew enough to get it off the branch.

"The clue is in the state . . ."

"We don't know the state, Harvey," Mom reminded me.

"I can figure it out, Mom. And when I do that, we can find the city. I'll be right back."

When I came back to the kitchen, I was carrying the atlas. I put it on the table and opened it to a map of the United States.

"See?" I pointed. "There are only three states that end in *ana* — Montana, Louisiana, and Indiana."

"I wouldn't exactly call that narrowing it down," Mom said.

"But it is, Mom," I explained. "There are state maps in our encyclopedia, with lists of all the cities. I'll look up Louisiana . . ."

"I'll take Montana," Mom said, getting right into the spirit of things.

". . . and I'll look up Indiana!" Nora exclaimed.

Wouldn't you know it would be Nora who found the city? I rescue a monkey, and she takes him over. I figure something out, and she finds the answer. Life is not fair, that's all I can say.

She shouted the name as soon as she spotted it.

"Vevay. Vevay, Indiana. Look. It's right here on the Ohio River, at the tip of the state."

And then, without any warning, she burst into tears.

Aloha, who had curled up in Nora's lap and fallen asleep while we were talking, woke up with a start. He took one look at the tears running down Nora's face and began to make little clicking sounds. Then he jumped up on the table, whisked across to Dad, snatched the handkerchief poking out of his jacket pocket, and scrambled back across the table to Nora. He wrapped himself around her shoulder and tried to wipe her tears away. That only made Nora cry harder.

"What's the matter with you?" I asked with exasperation. "One minute you're Sally Sunshine, and the next minute you're Maggie Miserable."

"It's Aloha," Nora sobbed. "Now that I've solved the puzzle we'll have to give Aloha back. I don't want to. He's mine."

I think if monkeys could cry, Aloha would have been sobbing by now, too. When the handkerchief didn't stop the flow of tears, he offered Nora his teddy bear.

"Cut that out," I yelled. I had a lump as big as a boulder in my own throat. Misery is sure contagious.

"Go splash some cold water on your face," Mom ordered. "Then come back here, Nora. We've got to talk."

The cold water must have helped, because when Nora came back to the table, she said immediately, "I'm sorry, Aunt Joy. I know we have to give Aloha back. It just hit me without my realizing it — that I really do have to give Aloha back to his owner, and that I'll never see him again."

The boulder in my throat grew bigger. I didn't want to part with Aloha either! So I got mad.

"You weren't the one who solved the puzzle," I reminded her. "It was my idea."

Chief Clark wasn't taking sides. He stood up and said, "Good work, kids. I'm proud of both of you." He turned to my dad. "I'll bypass the computers and put in a call to Vevay as soon as I get back to headquarters. In a town that size, the police will be able to fill in a name and address."

"Aren't we overlooking something, Oaty?" Mom asked in a quiet voice. "It's wonderful if we can discover where the monkey came from. But what about Harvey's crocodile man? He seems to want Aloha desperately. I have a feeling he'll be coming back."

"Not to worry," the Chief said, putting a comforting hand on my mom's shoulder. "We'll have an officer on guard at the front of the house, and one at the back. If that man comes back, he's most likely to get here when everyone is asleep. But we'll be ready for him."

"I have some ideas of my own about protecting this family when he returns," Dad said.

I did, too, but I didn't say anything just then. I wanted to confide my plan to Nora first. When I did, she held out her hand.

"Let's shake on it," she said. So we did. "It can't miss," she added. "If your dad agrees."

13
In which
Harvey uses his marbles

After Mrs. Motley left, taking Doolittle with her, Dad called us into the kitchen.

"Let's sit down and have a powwow," he said.

So we all gathered around the table and looked at him expectantly.

"I agree that the crocodile man is going to return. He'd be a fool if he tried to get in tonight, with the police on guard, but he seems extremely determined to get Aloha, so we have to be prepared."

"Can't we just leave it to the police?" Mom asked. "Suppose that awful man has a gun?"

"If we take him by surprise, he won't get a chance to use it. Now listen. I have a plan. It's simple, and it's foolproof."

Mom looked doubtful. "No plan is fool-proof, Thor. Something can always go wrong."

"Don't be such a worrywart," he told her, but he was too excited to be annoyed. "Come with me, and I'll show you exactly what I'm going to do."

So we trooped after my dad to the front door. He stepped back a couple of feet.

"I'm going to put a trip wire right across here." He swung his arm, pointing a finger from one side of the door to the other. "Not too close. Just enough space for him to come in before his feet catch the wire."

Nora was disappointed. "Is that it?"

I knew better. My dad has a complicated mind. Nora wouldn't know, of course. She only sees him on her short visits, but I have to live with him.

"Then what?" I asked.

Dad flashed me a grin of approval.

"I'm going to set up one of my cameras right about here." He stepped back several paces, held his hands about three feet apart, and measured a space between where he stood and the door.

Dad had that same gleam in his eye he gets when he thinks he's about to take the perfect picture, maybe even get it hung in a museum, or something.

"That's the plan? You're going to take a *picture* of him?" Mom was so irritated she started to leave.

"Yes, I am, Joy." The way he said that made Mom change her mind and come back.

"I'm setting the camera up with a strobe light . . ."

Mom and Nora looked puzzled, but I latched on to his scheme right away.

"Dad, that's terrific. You're going to blind him."

Nora was still puzzled, so I explained. "That strobe produces flashes of light that are so brilliant, you can't see when they explode in your face. Even when the light goes off, your eyes can't focus for quite a while."

"And," Dad added, "as an extra precaution, I'll rig the wire so a loud alarm will be set off at the same time."

Dad was not only going to blind the crocodile man, he was going to deafen him as well.

But Mom was still worried. "And then what? Are you planning to capture him yourself?"

Dad shook his head, but he looked a little regretful. "No. I promised Oaty I wouldn't try to be a hero. The second the police see the flash and hear the bell, they'll come in and nab him."

"He could come in the kitchen door," Nora said.

Dad smiled. "No way. We'll have the same setup there, too."

"Harvey has a good plan, too, Uncle Thor. Why don't you tell them, Harvey?"

I got a little mad. Why does she do that? I wanted to pick my own good time because I could see they thought my dad's idea was perfect. But I will say my parents are always willing to listen.

So I explained my idea. Mom didn't think it would work. Dad didn't think it would be needed. But they both agreed we could keep it as a back-up plan.

Dad got busy setting up his trap, and he didn't want any help. Nobody is allowed to touch his cameras or equipment, not even Mom.

We hadn't had lunch so Mom said she would treat us to a gourmet meal, but she wound up ordering pizza.

After lunch, Nora and I went upstairs to play the video game she had brought, then we went down to watch Dad, and finally we looked at TV. The day seemed to go on forever, and the night was even longer. Nobody wanted to go to bed, so we sat down at the head of the steps, with Butch stretched out, dead to the world. Aloha was fast asleep in Nora's bed.

In spite of ourselves, we all nodded off. After a while, Dad tapped us and said, with great disappointment, "It's two o'clock in the morning. We can go to bed. He won't be coming."

Then we heard it, a scuffing sound so soft, if Dad hadn't wakened us just then, we wouldn't have heard it. Butch heard it, too. He half opened one eye.

"It's him," Mom whispered. "But how?"

"It sounds as if he's right under us somewhere." Nora kept her voice low, too.

"The basement door!" I said. "We forgot about that. He must have sneaked in through a basement window while the cops weren't watching."

I felt sorry for my dad. He'd worked so hard setting up his trap. I thought he'd explode, because he has a really low boiling point. But instead, he touched my arm and told me, "Time for your back-up plan, Harvey."

I nodded. Quickly, but quietly, I tiptoed down the stairs and stopped halfway. I took a lot of marbles from my marble bag and scattered them on a few of the steps. Then I went back up on tiptoe again.

While I was busy with the marbles, Dad and Mom took Nora's fishing net out of the trash bag. Mom and Nora held it up on one side of the stairway. When I came back, Dad and I held the other side.

Butch stood up, ready to growl, but one sharp command from Dad and he dropped down and buried his nose in his outstretched paws.

We were ready and waiting when we heard the crocodile man stealing his way up the steps. He was so good, we wouldn't have heard him at all if we weren't straining to hear him.

Suddenly there was a shout, and the sound of a body hitting the steps. Dad flicked the light on, and we sent the net sailing down. It caught the crocodile man and wrapped itself around him.

Command or no, Butch couldn't hold back now. Barking, he went tearing down the steps. His barking changed to yelps as his paws hit the marbles. He went flying through the air, landing with a thump on the crocodile man at the foot of the stairway.

"Got you," Dad yelled.

"Watch the marbles, Dad," I warned as he was about to race down. So he just slid down the banister on one side, and Mom slid down on the other, with Nora and me following the same way.

We had no sooner reached the bottom of the stairway when one policeman came pounding in the front door, and the other one through the kitchen door. Hearing all the noise, they forgot about the trip wires. So the strobe lights flashed after all, the alarms rang, and the policeman were saying words I'm not supposed to know.

Dad untangled Butch, who was in a frenzy, while the crocodile man struggled furiously to get free of the net. Before long, the policemen reached us, blinking rapidly and shaking their heads to clear them. In minutes, they had the crocodile man clear of the net and in handcuffs, and out the front door on his way to jail.

You wouldn't believe how quiet the house felt after they were gone.

"I'm exhausted," Mom said. "I've got to get some sleep. Let's get to bed."

"I'll wait up," Dad told her. "Oaty said he'd call, no matter how late, to tell us about Aloha. And now, of course, with what he finds out about our crocodile man."

That settled it, of course. No one wanted to miss that call.

So once again we went to the kitchen. Mom made us all hot cocoa, the way I like it, with marshmallows floating on top. We all had a nice, warm, close-together feeling. So we talked a little, but not much, because all we really wanted to hear was the sound of the telephone ringing.

14
In which
the mystery is solved

The next morning was Saturday, which gave my mom and dad a free day. Even though we hadn't slept much, we were all up early, for we were going to drive to Vevay, Indiana.

"It's about a four-hour drive," Dad warned us. He can't seem to forget that when I was little, I used to ask "Are we there yet?" when we were only about five minutes away from home.

Nora was quiet. So was I. We both felt subdued now that we were actually on our way to return Aloha. Maybe he sensed our mood, because every now and then he studied our faces and seemed to frown.

If Mom and Dad noticed, they didn't say

anything, just chatted away to make the trip pass by more quickly.

"Imagine." Mom shook her head in disbelief. "I never dreamed there was such a thing as animal-napping."

That was what Chief Clark had told us when he stopped by instead of calling, since it was on his way home anyway.

"Your crocodile man is Hubert Strange. No, I'm not making that up," he said, when Dad repeated the name. "Also known as Harley Swift, and Henry Sharp, and Harry Seller."

"He's not from around here, is he?" Dad wanted to know. "Joy thought he might be because he came to the house pretending to be a health official, and had what appeared to be an official uniform . . ."

"We tracked down the place he rented the stuff from, that costume house over on Denver Road. The one that supplies the little theater group when they put on their plays . . ." The Chief pursed his lips. "They never even asked why he wanted the uniform . . . oh, well."

Dad was still curious. "What was he doing out at our place?"

"Seems he hadn't locked the back door of his van and it was beginning to swing open. So he stopped and went around in back to shut it. But meanwhile the monkey had figured out how to open his cage and slipped through the door just as Strange came over. The monkey took off, and that's how he found his way up your tree. Of course, Strange wasn't going to leave without that little creature if he could help it."

"But why?" Mom asked. "Was he a pet?"

"No," Nora said at once. "He never had a pet in his life. He's too mean!"

"He's the ringleader of a gang that steals valuable animals —"

"I knew it. I just knew it." Nora sounded triumphant.

The Chief went right on explaining — "and sells them to kennels, or experimental labs, and even individuals. Strange stole Aloha for a man with a handicapped son who promised Strange a lot of money if he could find a trained capuchin monkey right away."

I was shocked. "That man would buy Aloha even if he knew it was stolen from another handicapped person?"

Nora was shocked, too. "That's awfibble. What a rotten thing to do."

Mom looked sad. "People get desperate, Harvey." I could tell she felt sorry for the father, whoever he was, who had a handicapped son. Mom does that a lot — sees both sides of a story, I mean. "Desperate people take desperate measures," she said.

Chief Clark also mentioned that the crocodile man — I guess I should think of him as Hubert Strange — had a record. "As long as your arm, Thor," was the way he put it.

"Did you find out about the hypodermic?" Mom wanted to know.

The Chief nodded. "He just wanted to tranquilize Aloha, put him back in his cage, and take off. He wouldn't have killed Aloha. That little monkey is too valuable."

"So the mystery is solved." Nora sighed.

I knew how she felt. We were all glad it was over, and that the crocodile man had been caught. But it sure had been exciting while it was happening. Playing a video game didn't begin to compare with it.

"And with the help of Chief Clark," Mom rounded out our adventure, "and the police in

Vevay, Indiana, the real owner of Aloha has been found."

"And we're going there to return Aloha to her personally," I said with satisfaction.

Nora sighed again. "I do like stories to have a happy ending. Although," she added somewhat wistfully, "it would be a happier ending if there was just some way I could keep Aloha."

"Now, Nora," Mom told her. "We've been all over that."

"Besides," I reminded her. "You know your mom wouldn't let you have a monkey."

"How do you know?" she flashed back. "Nobody could not love Aloha, not even my mother."

To prove it, she nuzzled Aloha. Then she stroked Aloha on the belly while Aloha looked off into the distance and probably dreamed he was in monkey heaven.

And now here we all were, in the car, with Aloha and his teddy bear wrapped in the white blanket, cradled in Nora's arms, and Nora silently staring out the car window.

I was even feeling a little resentful toward Aloha. Why did he have to be so appealing?

Why couldn't he just be a plain old monkey instead of an animal you just wanted to love to pieces?

Mom turned around, stared at us, then nodded her head in Nora's direction. I got the message. She wanted me to distract Nora. So I did.

"Tell you what, Nora. Let's play 'my name is.' You can start if you want to."

If Nora knew what I was up to, she pretended not to notice. She began, "My name is Agatha. I live in Atlanta. I eat avocados. I sleep on an accordion. I ride on an albatross . . ."

When we got to *h*, I announced that I was hungry. So we stopped off at a diner and filled up with hamburgers.

At the table, Dad filled in the strange clue about the address on Aloha's collar. He took a paper napkin and sketched it in as we remembered it, like this:

$$\begin{array}{ccc} & \text{ort} & \\ & \text{x} & \text{0} \\ \text{V va} & & \text{ana} \end{array}$$

It was still just a jumble of letters until

Dad's pen moved again. Then he showed us what he had written.

> Zena Worth
> P.O. Box 220
> Vevay, Indiana

"We have her street address, so we won't have any trouble finding her," Dad told us.

I thought maybe he would speed up a little when we went back to the car, to get us to Vevay faster. But he never went over the speed limit anywhere. He's a man who practices what he preaches.

We didn't know what to expect when we met Zena Worth. All we knew was that she was handicapped. Paralyzed, Chief Clark said, and in a wheelchair.

I was worried about meeting her. I was afraid I would stare, or say something dumb and hurt her feelings.

Nora must have been sharing my thoughts because she turned to me and whispered, "Harvey, maybe we ought to wait in the car when we get there."

I made up my mind. "No. We can't. We have to meet her." I was glad we did.

Zena Worth turned out to be the best ex-
perience of my life!

15
In which
a story ends

Zena Worth looked a little older than Geor-geann. She had short, black hair that curled around her head, a round, rosy face, with deep dimples in her cheeks, and large, black eyes with a sparkle in them that didn't quit. When she laughed, which she did a lot, you could tell the laugh just welled up from every part of her body.

She sure had laughed with delight when she saw Aloha. And Aloha had the look of someone who had come home. He wrapped himself around Zena's shoulder, put his head lovingly against hers, and "hooo'd" like mad. It was clear to all of us, even to Nora, that this was where Aloha truly belonged.

Zena could tell her cheerfulness surprised

us. "You were expecting a gloomy Gus." She grinned at us. She didn't wait for an answer. "Because I can't use my arms and legs, and because I have to depend on a monkey. Well, I was a gloomy Gus for a long time after my accident. I was angry. I hated the way I was. I made everybody around me suffer, especially my mother."

I looked at Mrs. Worth, who was listening as if she had never heard any of this before. She was a tall woman, with dark hair streaked with gray, a face that looked severe until she smiled, and a watchful expression in her brown eyes.

"Then two things happened. My mother let me know I was making life unbearable for both of us. She said I had to start accepting the fact that this was what my life would be from now on, and I better adjust to it."

"I told her we didn't have quitters in our family," Mrs. Worth put in.

"And she got me Aloha," Zena explained.

"I work as a cook in the school cafeteria. While I'm away during the day, Aloha takes care of Zena's needs," Mrs. Worth told us.

Aloha clapped his hands, almost as if to

show us he knew they were talking about him.

"It took a while before Aloha and I got used to doing things together," Zena admitted.

"And Aloha had to learn the code," Nora said.

"How did you know about the code?" Zena was surprised.

"We found it," I said. "The whistle, too. In Aloha's collar."

Mom said, "I hope you don't mind my asking. Why would you put the whistle and code in the collar? You couldn't . . . I mean . . ." She stopped talking. I could tell Mom was embarrassed.

"That wasn't for me." Zena laughed. "Much good it would do me. That was Mom's idea."

Mrs. Worth took over. "When we first got Aloha, I was very nervous. I was sure I would forget the code. So I pasted copies of it up on the cabinets, kept one in my wallet, and for extra safety, had a special collar made for Aloha and slipped a whistle and code in it as well. See, I was the one who worked with Aloha in the beginning."

"And then," Zena interrupted, "we got a laser beam rod a little while ago, so we never used the code again after that."

"I took down all the codes, threw away the one in my wallet, and forgot about Aloha's collar."

"Lucky you did," my dad commented, "because that's what helped us find you."

Zena showed us how the laser beam worked. She held a long thin rod in her mouth. When she pressed down on it, a light came on. Then she flashed the light on a book. Aloha got the book, put it on a reading stand and opened it. Each time Zena flashed the beam, Aloha turned a page. When Zena dropped the rod, Aloha picked it up and stuck it back in Zena's mouth.

Dad had been looking around during the demonstration. Now he pointed to some equipment on a long table pushed against a wall. "Who's the ham radio operator?" he asked with interest.

"Zena," Mrs. Worth said promptly. "It was her idea."

"I decided if I couldn't get out into the world, I'd bring the world to me," Zena said, beaming. "Now I have friends all over the world. Want to see how it works?"

Mrs. Worth pushed Zena's wheelchair to the table. Aloha immediately sprang up there and waited expectantly. Mrs. Worth put the laser beam rod in Zena's mouth. Zena directed it toward a switch. Aloha touched it and a red light glowed immediately.

"That's the power switch," Dad explained to us. "With the power on, Zena can start broadcasting."

"Isn't that too hard for Aloha?" Nora worried. I wondered if she was still having a last minute hope that somehow when we left, Aloha would come with us.

Mrs. Worth smiled. "The switches are all touch-sensitive. That's why Aloha can operate them so easily. One of the panels is for reception. The first switch turns it on."

Zena shifted the beam to another switch. When Aloha touched it, another small light glowed red, and a blast of sound blared out. Aloha howled at the noise, and waited for the laser beam light to move on. When it did, he pressed the next switch, which turned on an orange light. The sound level dropped.

"That's the volume control," I told Nora. "Just like on our TV set."

Finally, Aloha touched the last switch. That light was green.

"Now I can select the band I want to talk on — *A*, *B*, or *C*," said Zena.

"I don't understand any of this," Nora told her.

"It looks a whole lot more complicated than it is. Think of it as a telephone. You talk in one end, and listen at the other." Zena noticed the way Dad looked at the equipment. "Want to try it?" she asked.

Dad's face brightened. In a few minutes, he was beaming. "I've got Brazil!" he shouted.

Zena's mother and my mom were talking in one corner of the room. My dad was occupied in another. So Zena suggested we wheel her next to the window and talk. She was smart. She knew that something was bothering Nora.

"You have a question?"

Nora nodded. "When you're talking . . . the people you talk to, they can't see you . . ." She stopped.

"You want to know if I tell them I'm

handicapped. Sometimes yes. Sometimes no. Why?"

"Would they talk to you if they knew you were, well, different?" Nora asked in a low voice.

"Maybe. Maybe not. Listen, Nora. You don't have to be handicapped to be different. Maybe some of the people I talk to are different in their own way, too. Sometimes being different is just the way other people see us, or think about us. I know there are those who can't accept what I am. But the thing is, *I* can accept me. Think about that, Nora."

"I wish I had someone like you to talk to," Nora blurted, then looked embarrassed.

"Hey! Great idea! I send out letter cassettes all the time. Just stick my laser rod in my mouth, will you?"

When Nora did so, Zena directed a beam at a tape recorder on the table. When Aloha saw the beam, he turned on the recorder, leaping back when a voice came on.

"Hi, there, Zena. What's cooking in your neck of the woods? By the way . . ."

Aloha turned the recorder off at another

beam from the laser. When Zena turned her head a bit to one side, Aloha came, took the rod out of Zena's mouth, and put it down carefully on the tray across Zena's lap.

"Can you get hold of a tape recorder?" Zena asked.

"My father has one. He'd let me use it." Nora couldn't seem to believe what Zena was saying. "You mean you'd send *me* . . . but you're grown-up, and I'm only ten."

"What's that between friends? And friends talk to each other, Nora. Everybody needs someone to talk to, do you understand?"

Nora nodded.

"Besides," Zena went on, with a laugh. "I have a feeling I'll be getting some very interesting tapes from you."

When it was time to leave, it hit us again that we were leaving Aloha behind. Nora cuddled him in her arms, and whispered things we couldn't hear. Aloha looked sad. At least I think he did. Maybe I was just giving him our own human emotions.

Zena was quick to understand.

"Hey, guys! Listen. I'll have my mother

take snaps of Aloha and send them to you. That way you'll still be in touch with him, okay?"

That promise made it easier for Nora and me to say goodbye to Aloha. He wouldn't let my mom take his teddy bear away. Secretly I was glad. Maybe it would remind him of us somehow.

In the car, I could tell that Nora was thinking — hard. She turned to me finally, her eyes large and serious in her owl face.

"Do you like Mrs. Motley?" she asked.

"Mrs. Motley?" I repeated, with surprise.

"Do you like her?" Nora was insistent about getting an answer.

"Sure I do. She's weird, but she's interesting."

"What about Chief Clark? You think he's different?"

"You better believe it," I told her. "And before you ask, yes, I like him, too."

I wondered where Nora was headed with all her questions.

"And *I'm* different. So tell me the truth, Harvey. Do you like me at all?"

I think what I said next was as much a

surprise to me as it was to her. Without even taking time to think about it, I said, "Sure I do. We've had a lot of fun together."

What a strange thing for me to discover!

My own cousin was good company. Georgeann would never believe it if I told her.

I started to laugh.

Nora grinned at me.

"That's splendific, Harvey! That's absolutely, one hundred percent splendific!"